PENGUIN CORE CONCEPTS

Dear Educators, Parents, and Caregivers,

Welcome to Penguin Core Concepts! The Core Concepts program exposes children to a diverse range of literary and informational texts, which will help them develop important literacy and cognitive skills necessary to meet many of the Common Core State Standards (CCSS).

The Penguin Core Concepts program includes twenty concepts (shown on the inside front cover of this book), which cover major themes that are taught in the early grades. Each book in the program is assigned one or two core concepts, which tie into the content of that particular book.

Bizz and Buzz Make Honey Buns covers the concepts Friendship and Problem Solving. This book can be used to expose students to text that covers the social-emotional concept Friendship, as recommended in the CCSS for Speaking and Listening. By learning appropriate behaviors for interacting with friends, students can develop important skills such as respect, caring, and cooperation. The concept Problem Solving can help students develop important cognitive skills necessary to meet many of the CCSS, such as how to apply problem-solving skills to decipher unfamiliar vocabulary. After you've read the book, here are some questions/ideas to get your discussions started:

- Bizz and Buzz mistake the word *flour* for the word *flower*. Use this as a springboard to discuss homophones.

- Talk about Bizz and Buzz's problem-solving skills. How do they find the right ingredients to use?

- Bizz and Buzz are friends. Discuss the qualities of a good friend.

Above all, the books in the Penguin Core Concepts program have engaging stories with fantastic illustrations and/or photographs, and are a perfect way to instill the love of reading in a child!

Bonnie Bader, EdM
Editor in Chief, Penguin Core Concepts

Bizz & Buzz
make honey buns

To Joe, Rachelle, and Brandy,
for putting up with my cooking all these years—DL

To Pauline & David—M

GROSSET & DUNLAP
Published by the Penguin Group
Penguin Group (USA) LLC, 375 Hudson Street, New York, New York 10014, USA

USA | Canada | UK | Ireland | Australia | New Zealand | India | South Africa | China

penguin.com
A Penguin Random House Company

Text copyright © 2014 by Dee Leone. Illustrations copyright © 2014 by Penguin Group (USA) LLC. All rights reserved. Published by Grosset & Dunlap, a division of Penguin Young Readers Group, 345 Hudson Street, New York, New York 10014. GROSSET & DUNLAP is a trademark of Penguin Group (USA) LLC. Manufactured in China.

Library of Congress Cataloging-in-Publication Data is available.

ISBN 978-0-448-47927-9 (pbk)   10 9 8 7 6 5 4 3 2 1
ISBN 978-0-448-47928-6 (hc)   10 9 8 7 6 5 4 3 2 1

To: Avani
Happy birthday!

Bizz & Buzz
make honey buns

by Dee Leone
illustrated by Maritie

Dee Leone

Grosset & Dunlap
An Imprint of Penguin Group (USA) LLC

Bizz and Buzz were best friends.

They played together.

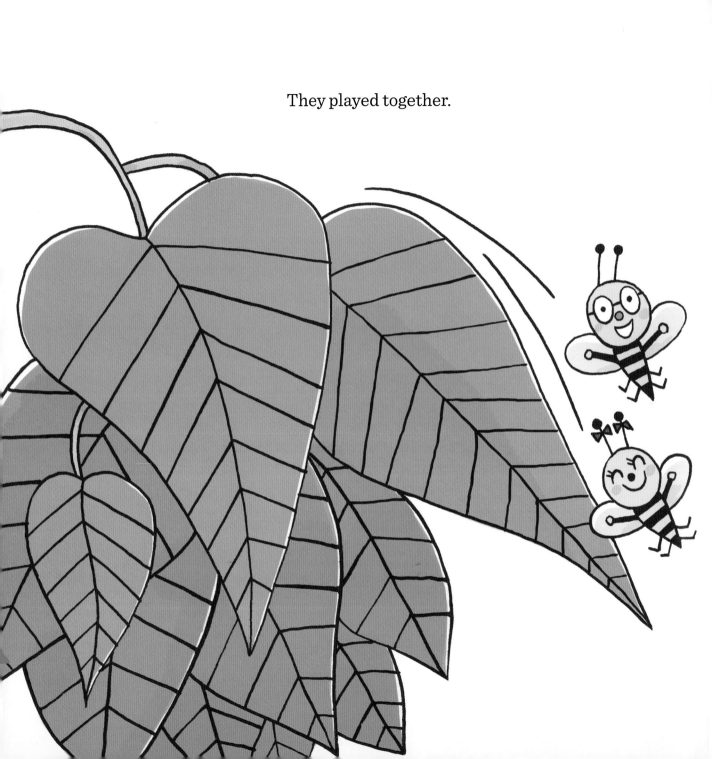

They sang together.

And they ate together.

One day, Bear invited them over for honey buns.
"These are delicious. Can you tell us how to make one?"
asked Buzz.

Bear was always willing to help. "First, you need a little flour."
"Thank you, Bear. We know just where to look," said Bizz.

The bees flew to a garden. They saw some red roses.

"Will those work?" asked Buzz.

"No," answered Bizz. "Roses are too big.
Bear said we need a *little* flower."

They saw some purple tulips.
"What about those?" asked Buzz.
"Still too big," answered Bizz.

Buzz saw lots of little yellow flowers. "Look! Buttercups."

They landed on the smallest one.

"This one is perfect," said Bizz.

"Yes, it is a *little* flower," added Buzz.

They went back to their friend.

"We found a little flower," they told him.

"Good," said Bear. "Next, add water to the flour."

Bizz and Buzz flew off. But it started to rain!
So they hid under a mushroom.

"I hope this rain stops soon," said Bizz.
"Me too. I want to finish making our honey bun," added Buzz.

Finally, the rain stopped.

Bizz and Buzz flew back to the buttercup . . . their own *little* flower.

"How do we add water?" asked Buzz.

They thought and they thought.

Buzz got tired of thinking and splashed Bizz.
Suddenly, Bizz buzzed with excitement.
"Buzz, we don't need to add water to the
flower. The rain already did."

They went to see Bear again.
"Now add butter," he said.

Bizz and Buzz flew back to the buttercup . . .
their own *little* flower, the one with water on top.

"How do we add butter?" asked Bizz.

"Where do we even *find* butter?" wondered Buzz.

They thought and they thought.

Suddenly, Bizz buzzed with
excitement. "Buzz, this is a
buttercup. It already *has* butter."

"Oh, Bizz. You are so smart."

They visited Bear again.

"We have the flower. We have the water. We have the butter," bragged Buzz.

"Now knead it all together," Bear told them.

Bizz and Buzz flew back to the buttercup . . .
their own *little* flower, the one with water on top
and butter inside.

"It's time to need it all," said Bizz.

Buzz looked at the buttercup. "Little flower, we need you. We need you so much."

"Water, butter, we need you, too," added Bizz.

"Do you think that is enough needing?" asked Buzz.

"Yes. I'm hungry. Let's go."

Bear told them the next thing to do. "Now bake it."

Bizz and Buzz flew back to the buttercup . . . their own *little* flower, the one with water on top and butter inside, the one they needed so much.

"How can we bake it?" asked Buzz.

"We need something hot," Bizz said.

They thought and they thought.

They got hotter and hotter.

Bizz started to sweat. So did Buzz.

Suddenly, Bizz buzzed with excitement.

"The sun is baking it for us!" said Bizz.

The bees went back to Bear.

"The last thing you need to do is add some honey," said Bear.

That was easy for the bees. They knew just where to look!

They added the honey to the flower.

Then Bizz and Buzz looked at each other.

"It doesn't *look* like the honey buns Bear made," said Bizz.

"It doesn't *smell* like the honey buns Bear made," said Buzz.

"Maybe he used a different kind of flower," said Bizz.

Buzz was hungry. "Let's taste it, anyway."

"Mmm. Bear sure knows how
to make good honey buns," said Buzz.
Bizz licked up every last bit.
"And now we do, too."